E
PO

Poulet, Virginia

Blue Bug goes to the
library

# BLUE BUG GOES to the LIBRARY

By Virginia Poulet

Illustrated by Peggy Perry Anderson

 CHILDRENS PRESS, CHICAGO

*For a very special editor, Fran Dyra*

Library of Congress Cataloging in Publication Data

Poulet, Virginia.
  Blue Bug goes to the library.

  SUMMARY: Brief text and illustrations outline the
activities and materials available at a library.
    1. Libraries—Juvenile literature. [1. Libraries]
I. Anderson, Peggy Perry. II. Title.
Z665.5.P68      027.4      79-15219
ISBN 0-516-03430-8

    8 9 10 11 12 R 85 84

# At the library,
# Blue Bug can...

Once upon a time...

read story books,

# look at magazines,

START

7

listen to records and

tapes,

# see art and

13

14

things,

watch films,

# look at pictures,

use the dictionary,

ENCYCLOPED ENCYCLOPED ENCYCLOPED ENCYCLOPED ENCYCLOPED ENCYCLOPE

E    F    G    H    I    J

find answers,

listen to stories,

BORROWER'S CARD

NAME Blue Bug

ADDRESS ABC Avenue

CITY Bugville

CITY COUNTY LIBRARY

# use his library card to…

# take books home, and

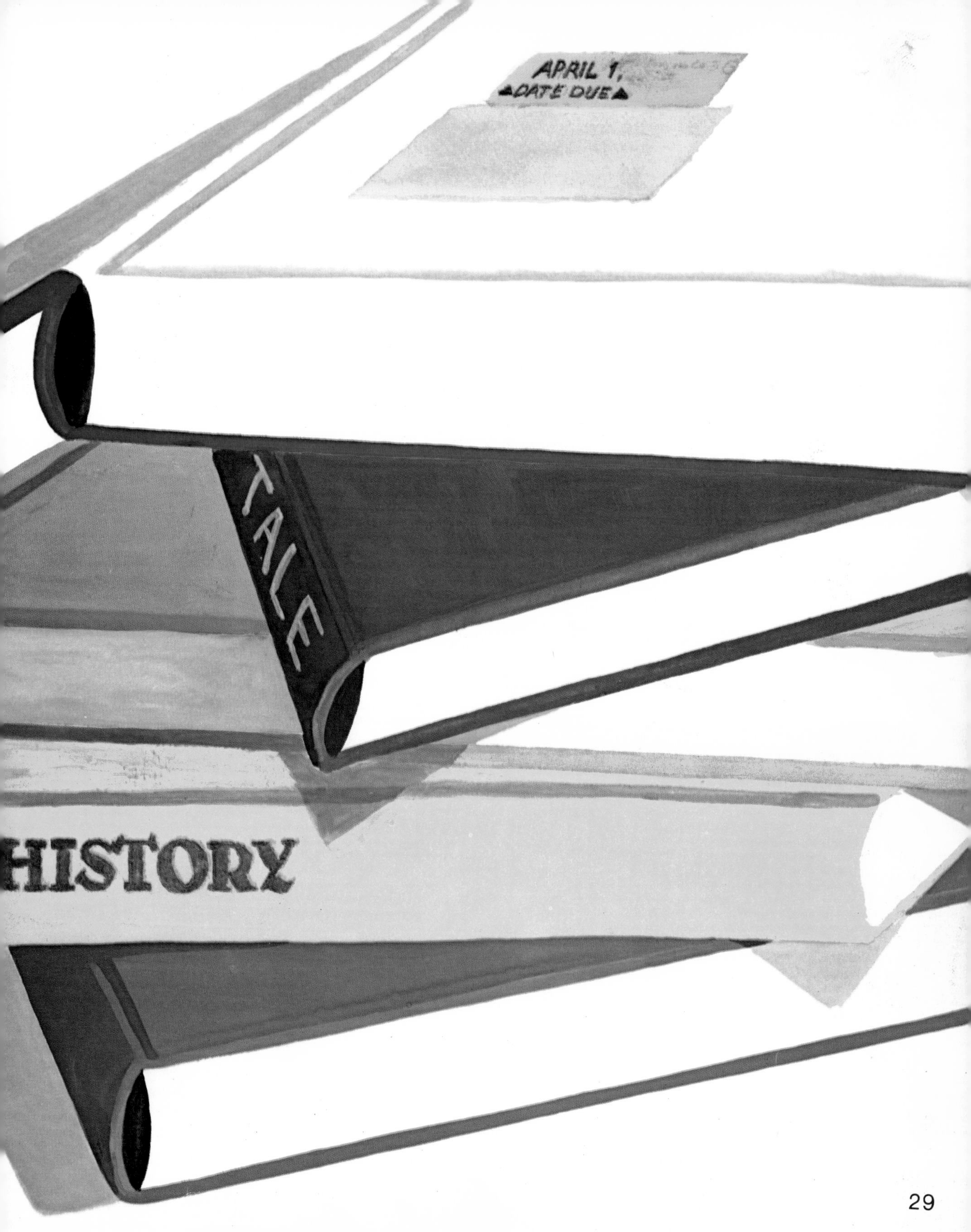

APRIL 1,
DATE DUE
TALE
HISTORY

visit his friend !

LIBRARIAN

Children's Book Week

Blue Bug giggles when
the librarian
calls him a bookworm!